"Hello? Hello? HELLO?"
Scooter was trying
to talk on the telephone.
He was trying to talk to Kermit.
But there was too much noise.

Miss Piggy was singing.
Gonzo was riding his motorbike.
Rowlf was playing the piano.
Fozzie Bear was telling jokes
and laughing as hard as he could.
The Muppets were getting ready
for their big new show.
It was opening that night.

Kermit's Mixed-up Message

by Joanne Barkan

illustrated by Lauren Attinello

SCHOLASTIC INC.

New York Toronto London Auckland Sydney

To Jon
—J.B.

ISBN 0-590-40704-X
Copyright © 1987 by Henson Organization Publishing, Inc.
All rights reserved. Published by Scholastic Inc. HELLO, READER is a trademark of Scholastic Inc.

12   11   10   9   8   7   6   5   4   3   2   1   7   8   9/8   0   1   2/9

Printed in the U.S.A.   09
First Scholastic printing, October 1987

Scooter hung up the phone.
"Quiet, everybody!" he called.
"I have something to tell you."
  The Muppets came over to hear Scooter.
"What's up?" asked Gonzo.

"I was talking to Kermit just now,"
said Scooter.
"He said there is a big problem.
The show might not go on tonight!"
The Muppets could not believe their ears.

"What is the big problem?"
Fozzie wanted to know.
"Well, that is another problem,"
said Scooter. "I don't know.
I could not hear too well.
There was too much noise.
Kermit said something.
It sounded like '*ite.*'

Then he said something else.

It sounded like '*all*.'

Ite. *All*. That is what I heard."

Ite. *All*.

What did Kermit really say?

"We must figure this out," said Rowlf.

"If we don't, there will be no show."

The Muppets were puzzled.

They were worried, too.

Miss Piggy went to her dressing room.

"*Ite. All*," she said to herself.

"Kermit must have been talking about me.
After all, he always talks about me."

Miss Piggy thought about it some more.

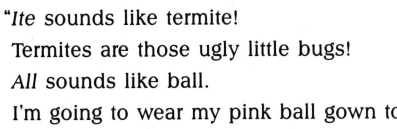

"*Ite* sounds like termite!
Termites are those ugly little bugs!
All sounds like ball.
I'm going to wear my pink ball gown tonight.
Oh, dear! I know what Kermit said.
There are termites in my ball gown!
Help!"

Miss Piggy ran over to her closet.
She pulled out her pink ball gown.
She shook it as hard as she could.
Then she looked at it again
and again and again.

"There are no termites
in this ball gown," she said.
"I should check my other costumes."
Miss Piggy pulled another costume
out of the closet —
and another and another.
Soon the floor was covered
with costumes.

Gonzo was having a snack —
oatmeal and peanuts.
He was thinking about Kermit, too.
"*Ite. All*," Gonzo said to himself.
"What does it mean? It's very strange.
So maybe it's about me!

Ite sounds like tight.

All sounds like fall."

Gonzo jumped up.

"Hold it!" he said.

"I know what Kermit said.

Something is wrong with my tightrope.

I could fall!"

Gonzo dashed to his tightrope.
"This really is a big problem,"
he said. "My tightrope act
is the best in the world.
The show cannot go on without me."

Gonzo began to check his tightrope.
He pulled it down.
He pulled it all around.
He made a big mess.

Rowlf, too, was thinking about
what Kermit said.
"*All*? *Ite*?" asked Rowlf.
"What does that sound like?"
He sat down at his small, white piano.
He wanted to think some more.
"Wait a minute!"
Rowlf's ears stood up. "*All* and *ite*.
That sounds like small and white!
There must be a problem
with my small, white piano!"
Rowlf opened up the piano.
He stuck his head inside.
"I must find out what is wrong,"
he said. "We can't do the show
without music."

Fozzie Bear was standing
in front of a mirror.
He wanted to practice his jokes.
But he was worried about the show.
"What did Kermit really say?"
he asked. "*Ite. Ite.*
That reminds me of my new joke.
It's about a kite in flight
on a bright night. Great joke!"
Fozzie thought about Kermit some more.
"*All. All.*
Now that reminds me
of another new joke.
It's about the chicken
that wanted to crawl
to the tall wall in a shawl.
Wocka, wocka!"

Suddenly, Fozzie looked upset.

"Oh, no!" he cried.

"Kermit was talking about my new jokes.
He does not like them.
I have to find some others right away!"
Fozzie ran to the bookcase.
He pulled down all his joke books.
He pulled down all the other books, too.
He was up to his knees in books.

Just then, Kermit walked in the door.
"Hello there," he called.
"Where is everybody?"
All the Muppets came running.
They were all talking at once.

"Kermit!" said Miss Piggy.
"There are no termites in my ball gown.
How could you say such a thing?"
"My tightrope is fine," said Gonzo.
"Don't worry. I'm not going to fall."

"What is wrong
with my small, white piano?"
asked Rowlf. "It looks fine to me."
"Kermit!" cried Fozzie.
"Why don't you like my new jokes?"

"Wait a minute!" said Kermit.

"What are you all talking about?"

"The big problem," said Scooter.

"We want to know what it is.

What did you say on the telephone?"

Kermit looked at his friends.
"I said the *lights* in the big *hall*
don't work."
The Muppets looked at each other.
Then they looked back at Kermit.
"The *lights* in the big *hall* don't work!
What can we do?"
"We have to fix them right away,"
said Kermit. "We can't do the show
in the dark."

The Muppets went to work.
They looked at all the lights.
They looked at all the wires.
Everyone helped.
They finally found the problem.

Before long, the lights in the
big hall went on.
"That is great!" said Kermit.
"Now let's put on our costumes.
On with the show!"

The Muppets' new show
was wonderful.
Piggy sang a song
about a handsome frog.
She wore her pink
ball gown. There was
not one termite in sight.
Gonzo rode his motorbike across the tightrope.
He didn't fall at all.

Rowlf played his small, white piano.
It sounded grand.
Fozzie told his joke about the kite.
Everyone liked it.
Then he told the one about the chicken
and the tall wall.
Everyone liked that one even more.

When the show ended,
people clapped and clapped.
They had a great time.
So did the Muppets.

And it all happened one night
under the bright lights
in the big hall.